THREE BLIND MICE
Round (or Canon) for Three Voices

Moderately quick

Twice through and finish at pause.

Complete Version of Ye
Three Blind Mice

By John W. Ivimey   *Illustrated by Walton Corbould*

FREDERICK WARNE

First published in 1904

27896

First published 1904 by Frederick Warne & Co. Ltd, London
New edition published 1979 by Frederick Warne (Publishers) Ltd, London
Copyright © 1979 Frederick Warne (Publishers) Ltd
Published in the USA by Frederick Warne & Co. Inc., New York 1979
Library of Congress Catalog Number: 79-65174

ISBN 0 7232 2256 8

Printed in Great Britain by Ashdown Printing Services Ltd
0202.479

Three Small Mice
Three Small Mice
Three Small Mice

Pined for some fun
Pined for some fun
Pined for some fun

They made up their minds to set out to roam;
Said they, "'Tis dull to remain at home,"
And all the luggage they took was a comb,
These three Small Mice.

Three Bold Mice
Three Bold Mice
Three Bold Mice

Came to an Inn
Came to an Inn
Came to an Inn

"Good evening, Host, can you give us a bed?"
But the Host he grinned and
he shook his head;

So they all slept out in a field instead,
These three Bold Mice.

Three Cold Mice
Three Cold Mice
Three Cold Mice

Woke up next morn
Woke up next morn
Woke up next morn

They each had a cold and swollen face,
Through sleeping all night in an open space;

So they rose quite early and left the place,
These three Cold Mice.

Three Hungry Mice
Three Hungry Mice
Three Hungry Mice

    Searched for some food
    Searched for some food
    Searched for some food

But all they found was a walnut shell
That lay by the side of a dried-up well;
Who had eaten the nut they could not tell,
    These three Hungry Mice.

Three Starved Mice
Three Starved Mice
Three Starved Mice

Came to a Farm
Came to a Farm
Came to a Farm

The Farmer was eating some bread and cheese;
So they all went down on their hands and knees,
And squeaked, "Pray, give us a morsel, please,"
These three Starved Mice.

Three Glad Mice
Three Glad Mice
Three Glad Mice

Ate all they could
Ate all they could
Ate all they could

They felt so happy they danced with glee;
But the Farmer's Wife came in to see
What might this merry-making be
Of three Glad Mice.

Three Poor Mice
Three Poor Mice
Three Poor Mice

    Soon changed their tone
    Soon changed their tone
    Soon changed their tone

The Farmer's Wife said, "What are you at,
And why were you capering round like that?
Just wait a minute: I'll fetch the Cat"

Oh dear! Poor Mice

Three Scared Mice
Three Scared Mice
Three Scared Mice

Ran for their lives
Ran for their lives
Ran for their lives

They jumped out on to the window ledge;
The mention of "Cat" set their teeth on edge;
So they hid themselves in the bramble hedge,
These three Scared Mice.

Three Sad Mice
Three Sad Mice
Three Sad Mice

What could they do?
What could they do?
What could they do?

The bramble hedge was most unkind:
It scratched their eyes and made them blind,

And soon each Mouse went out of his mind,
These three Sad Mice.

Three Blind Mice
Three Blind Mice
Three Blind Mice

See how they run
See how they run
See how they run

They all ran after the Farmer's Wife,
Who cut off their tails with the carving knife.
Did you ever see such a sight in your life
As three Blind Mice?

Three Sick Mice
Three Sick Mice
Three Sick Mice

Gave way to tears
Gave way to tears
Gave way to tears

They could not see and they had no end;
They sought a Chemist and found a Friend

He gave them some "Never too late to mend,"
These three Sick Mice.

Three Wise Mice
Three Wise Mice
Three Wise Mice

Rubbed rubbed away
Rubbed rubbed away
Rubbed rubbed away

And soon their tails began to grow,
And their eyes recovered their sight, you know;
They looked in the glass and it told them so,
These three Wise Mice.

Three Proud Mice
Three Proud Mice
Three Proud Mice

Soon settled down
Soon settled down
Soon settled down

The name of their house I cannot tell,
But they've learnt a trade and are doing well.

If you call upon them, ring the bell
Three times twice.

2

2

1

'98